Mama's Milk

SEA LION AND PUP

WITHDRAWN

BY Michael Elsohn Ross • ILLUSTRATIONS BY Ashley Wolff

TRICYCLE PRESS
Berkeley/Toronto

Cuddle little baby warm and tight
Mama's going to feed you day and night.

PIG AND PIGLETS

She'll fatten you up in a sunny pig sty.

MARE AND FOAL

She'll grow you up strong under the morning sky.

MONKEY AND INFANT

Mama's going to nurse you high up in a tree.

ELEPHANT AND CALF

Mama's going to nurse you down low by her knees.

Hang with your mama in a cave dark and cool.

RIVER OTTER AND PUP

Stay with your mama by a fishy pool.

She'll watch over you in a deep, soft home.

KANGAROO AND JOEY

She'll be there for you whenever you roam.

Sweet little baby, be still for a while.

Let mama feed you under her smile.

ARMADILLO AND PUPS

You can curl up with mama in a safe, dry furrow.

COYOTE AND PUPS

You can snuggle up to her in a secret burrow.

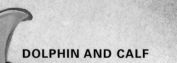

DOLPHIN AND CALF

Mama's going to swim as you sip and ride.

WHALE AND CALF

Mama's going to float as you nurse by her side.

Fill your tummy while mama snores.

Dine in peace in the dusky outdoors.

HAMSTER AND PUPS

You can snack at night in a cozy bed.

CAT AND KITTENS

You can wiggle all together when you are fed.

Cuddle little baby, take a rest
Fall asleep on mama's breast.

Sea lion mamas leave their pups for two to four days to catch fish, then nurse for two to three days.

Monkeys can nurse infants for a year or longer.

Puggles lick milk from patches on the mama platypus.

The biggest piglets nurse lowest on their mother's belly.

Female bats roost together while nursing.

Mama's milk helps to protect babies from common diseases.

Foals nurse every thirty minutes.

Calf elephants drink from mama for two to five years.

Otter pups nurse for seven weeks.

Kangaroo milk is pink.

Mama's milk enhances babies' brain development.

A mother whale squirts milk into her calf's mouth.

Kittens knead their mama's nipples to get the milk flowing.

Papa coyotes feed the mama while she is busy nursing.

Cubs nurse from mama bear while she sleeps through the winter.

Normally nocturnal, raccoon mamas often forage in daytime while nursing.

Armadillo pups nurse for two months.

A breastfeeding mama gets more sleep.

A dolphin calf holds its breath while feeding underwater.

Hamster pups nurse for three weeks.

For more breastfeeding inspiration, visit www.promom.org/101/

To my grandniece, amazing Emma Jeanne. —MER

For my mother, Deane, who nursed me.
And with thanks to the beautiful Tu family. —AW

Text copyright © 2007 by Michael Elsohn Ross
Illustrations copyright © 2007 by Ashley Wolff

TRICYCLE PRESS
an imprint of Ten Speed Press
PO Box 7123
Berkeley, California 94707
www.tricyclepress.com

Design by Susan Van Horn
Typeset in Sabon, Universe, and Wendy
The illustrations in this book were rendered in gouache.

Library of Congress Cataloging-in-Publication Data

Ross, Michael Elsohn, 1952-
Mama's milk / by Michael Elsohn Ross ; illustrated by Ashley Wolff.
p. cm.
Summary: Illustrations and rhyming text portray baby mammals nursing.
ISBN-13: 978-1-58246-181-6
ISBN-10: 1-58246-181-3
[1. Breastfeeding—Fiction. 2. Mammals—Fiction. 3. Animals—Infancy—Fiction. 4. Parental behavior in animals—Fiction. 5. Stories in rhyme.] I. Wolff, Ashley, ill. II. Title.
PZ8.3.R7432Mam 2007
[E]--dc22
2006020873

First Tricycle Press printing, 2007
Printed in Singapore

2 3 4 5 6 — 11 10 09 08 07